Imaginals!®

Ken Eichenbaum, *Visualist* • **Wayne Arihood,** *Versist*
Sher Schachameyer, *Illustrator*

Published by Litterati Publishing

Especially for James, Alexis,

Brandon, Benny, Ian, Joshua,

Rachel and Shea

Request for permission to make copies
of any part of the work should be mailed
to Litterati Publishing, 9470 N. Broadmoor
Road, Milwaukee, Wisconsin USA 53217.

ISBN No.: 0-9620271-8-9

Designed by Sher Schachameyer
Published by Litterati Publishing
Printed in China

We were warned it might happen...all those scientists and technicians meddling with DNA and cybernetics. Soon they'll be hard at work figuring out how to combine *living animals* with *inanimate objects*. Just think what fearsome creatures they might produce.

We believe the assignment ought to be given to the artist and the poet, instead. Chances are they could conceive a far more imaginative herd of hybrids.

A sort of zoo of the mind.

That is exactly what happened when Ken Eichenbaum, the idea person; Wayne Arihood, the versist; and Sher Schachameyer, the illustrator, got together to breed their own designer menagerie. The results: *Imaginals.*®

Of course they had extraordinary raw materials to work with. Consider the rich innovation inherent in a waddly round penguin, or a lumbering brown hippopotamus, or a gawky bearded moose, or any of ten thousand other two-, four-, or no-legged beasts. The supply is as endless as it is creative.

Inanimate objects are nearly as fascinating. Think of a cylindrical writing instrument with its own internal ink supply; or a rubber thingy that can wipe rain off a windshield; or tiny little gears that you wear on your wrist so you know when it's time to come home for dinner.

It's fun to see just where the technological revolution would be if it were propelled not by scientists, but by the fertile minds of Ken, Wayne and Sher. Sharing our ecospace with *Imaginals* might make our planet a nicer place to visit.

1

Forkupine

If you want to tell the story
Of the Forkupine,
You've got to start it out, of course,
With, "Once upon a Tine..."

Carpsichord - A combination of *Carp* (a kind of fish) and *Harpsichord,* (an old-fashioned kind of tinkly sounding piano).

Norway - A frosty country nearly surrounded by water.

Fjord - A deep valley in the mountains where the ocean has come in to fill it up. If you want to sound like a real Norwegian person you must pronounce the J in fjord like Y (fyord).

Lyric - With feeling.

Glissandoing - A sound made by whipping your thumb quickly up or down the piano keys until it hurts.

Dorsal - The tush end of a fish. That's where the dorsal fin sticks up.

Aquatic - *Aqua* means water in another language. *Aquatic* means water-like. An aquabatic fish would be one that swings on an underwater trapeze.

Scales - Can be either musical notes or the rough outside of a fish. You can also weigh yourself by standing on a scale, but you should never stand on a carp.

School - If you're a boy or a girl, it's where you go to learn. If you're a fish, it's the gang you swim around with.

Improvise - Make stuff up as you go along.

Carnegie - A famous and fancy place in New York where good musicians go to play.

Carpsichord

Deep in Norway's cold Fjord
Lives the lyric Carpsichord.
Glissandoing her dorsal sails,
Playing her aquatic scales.
She's been to school. This fish is wise.
She's always one to improvise.
And that is why one day you'll see
A Carpsichord at Carnegie.

Kangaruler - A combination of *Kangaroo* (which is an animal that has large hind legs for hopping and lives in a country called "Australia") and *Ruler* (which is a stick with numbers that you use to measure things).

Aussie - A name given to people (or Imaginals) who live in Australia.

Marsupial - A creature whose Momma carries her babies around in a built-in tummy pouch. This is especially handy if she has to go shopping.

Vertical - Means straight up and down. If "vertical" isn't fancy enough for you, try saying "perpendicular" which means about the same thing.

Kangaruler

This Aussie marsupial's main source of pleasure
Is looking for items to count or to measure.
How many, how wide, or how tall, or how deep?
She hops and then measures each vertical leap.
If you have a sister, and you'd like to fool her,
Ask her, "How many feet on a Kangaruler?"

Caterputer- A combination of *Caterpillar* and *Computer*.

Predecessor - Like Grandpa and Grandma, a predecessor is someone who was here before you came along.

Megabytes - In computer language this means a big number; a million or more.

Interleaves - Hardly anyone knows what interleaves are, but because it is a computer word and also sounds like leaves (on which you often see caterpillars), it seemed like a good place for the word. Also, it rhymes with achieves.

Mega-gigahertz - More computer talk; this time meaning how fast a computer can do things.

Caterputer

The Caterputer has no fuzz
Like his predecessor does.
His visions come in colored lights.
He chews his food in megabytes.
He's so advanced he now achieves
His nourishment through interleaves.
No longer humps along in spurts,
Now screams at mega-gigahertz.

Hippoteapotamus -
A combination of
Hippopotamus (a big, roly-poly
beast from Africa who loves to
swim) and *Teapot* (a pot to
make tea in).

Nostril - One nostril is one
nose hole. Most of us have
two, which helps when we
have a cold.

Steeping - Putting hot water
and dry tea leaves together
and waiting for good-tasting
tea to happen. Sometimes this
is called *brewing* tea.

Hippoteapotamus

To live under water would seem to a lot of us
Unpleasant, but not for the Hippoteapotamus.
She raises one nostril and one eye for peeping, see?
Thus leaving the rest for the business of steeping tea.

High Tension Lion - This is a combination of *Lion* (a big furry cat) and *High Tension* which is used to describe fat wires that carry a lot of electricity.

Zillion - A made-up number meaning a lot more than you could count, even if you stayed up all night with the light on.

Ergs - A term scientists use to measure how much work is being done. We have a cousin named Valerie who does no ergs after school and on weekends.

Amps, Ohms, Wattage, Voltage - These are all mysterious words having to do with electricity. If you want to know their real meaning, you have to ask an electrician or visit your dictionary.

High Tension Lion

The High Tension Lion is plugged in, but nervous
That someone will cut off his zillion amp service.
His power could light up a town if he weren't
Concerned about hoarding his leftover current.
He lives for his ergs and his ohms and his wattage
With never a thought for a vine-covered cottage.
So don't try to make him a pal or a chum
'Cause all you'll get back is a high-voltage hum.

Pogo Stork - This is a combination of *Pogo Stick* (a pole with a spring on one end so you can bounce on it for fun) and *Stork* (a long-legged bird that some people used to say brought new babies to their mothers).

Grace - When something is done smoothly and well. Clumsy Aunt Grace really should have been named Aunt Stumble.

Poise - When something is done smoothly and well without falling down. If you pass a glass of orange juice to your sister without spilling it on her lap, you have poise.

Pogo Stork

How do you think a Pogo Stork
Could make a living in New York?
He would, with grace and lots of poise,
Deliver bouncing baby boys.

Yarn Owl - A combination of *Owl*, a supposedly wise old bird who hoots, and a ball of *Yarn*, which is not known for being smart, but when untangled can make a warm pair of mittens. The joke is that there is an owl called a Barn Owl, so barn and yarn are switched around to entertain people who are easily amused. This is often called a "pun".

Mesmerize - This means to put you in a trance which is like being asleep and awake at the same time. Are you ever mesmerized in school?

Spell - A spell is like a charm or a fantasy. Experienced witches and hypnotists who know their business can put you under their spell and make you cackle like a hen, but they cannot make you lay eggs.

Philosophy - The answer you get when you finish the following sentence: "The reason I do the things I do is because I believe. . ."

Bliss - Another word for joy or happiness. When your dentist says you have no cavities, you should be in bliss.

Reminisce - To sit back and try to remember all the things that have ever happened to you. Uncle Clayton, who used to be a sailor, likes to reminisce about all the faraway places he visited. Aunt Agnes says he never takes her anyplace.

Yarn Owl

The Yarn Owl, with his starey eyes,
Has the power to mesmerize.
You can't resist his spell when he
Unravels his philosophy.
He'll tangle you in knots of bliss
When he begins to reminisce.

Alarmadillo - This is a combination of *Armadillo* (a small animal that loves to live in Texas near the highways) and *Alarm,* which is a bell that warns you that something is wrong.

Trespassers - People who go into someone else's yard, especially when the owner doesn't want them to go there.

Disasters - Bad things that can happen and maybe end up busting your stuff. Like a tornado.

Alarmadillo

The Alarmadillo is always on guard

To tell you if trespassers come in your yard.

He's always alert to the danger of fires,

Of high winds or waters, or natural-born liars.

He's funny to look at. His outside is brittle.

His nose is real hard and his legs are real little.

And high on his back are the bells that he rings

To warn of disasters and burglars and things.

Windshield Viper - A combination of *Windshield Wiper* (the thing on a car's window that is used when it rains) and *Viper* (sometimes called a Pit Viper, which is a yucky snake whose bite will make you sick).

Aptly Fitted - This means to be very good at something. A camcorder is aptly fitted to make videos.

Pitted - This means to have rough, raggedy dents all over. The floor in our kitchen is pitted because Uncle Marvin insists on wearing his spiked baseball shoes when he cooks so he doesn't slip on any sauce he might spill. (A fellow we know who works with snakes at the zoo told us that a real pit viper has two pits, one on each side of his head. But he doesn't have armpits).

Windshield Viper

The Windshield Viper's a charming guy.

He'll keep your window clear and dry.

For this task he's aptly fitted.

Especially if your windshield's pitted.

Fountain Penguin - This is a combination of *Fountain Pen* (a writing instrument) and *Penguin* (a roly-poly, short-legged bird who lives real far south, and also in zoos up north). A fountain pen is what people used before ballpoint or felt-tip pens were invented. In the olden days you wouldn't throw away your fountain pen when it ran out of ink. You would refill it from a bottle of blue or black ink. But you would have to be careful not to overfill it, or...*oops!*

Fountain Penguin

The Fountain Penguin's
A cute little squirt.
But just like his brother,
He'll leak in your shirt.

Gazebra - A combination of *Zebra* (an animal that looks like a horse with black and white stripes) and *Gazebo* (a tiny house without walls that you can build in your yard for sitting in).

Lurk - To try not to attract attention. You might lurk near the place where Mom keeps the cookies, and then grab one when she's not looking.

Harbor - Sometimes a place where boats are tied up, but here it means to have or to keep something. Melanie harbors a deep desire to squirt her little brother with the garden hose.

Quirk - A strange little thing that some people might do that makes them interesting, but that they might want to hide. Uncle Hank's quirk is to eat barbequed ribs in bed at night. Cousin Agnes likes to spit watermelon seeds at the mailman.

Gazebra

Don't see the Gazebra out in the yard.
She thinks that her stripes make finding her hard.
She hates to be caught while attempting to lurk.
But who doesn't harbor a similar quirk?

Moosepaper - A combination of *Moose* (a big four-legged animal that lives in the woods up north) and a *Newspaper* (you know what that is. It's where you find the comics).

Motto - In New York City there is a famous newspaper whose motto is "All the News That's Fit To Print." In our poem, we played around with those words to make a "pun".

Red - Here's another pun. We're playing with the word "Red" and another word that sounds just like it - "Read" - as in, "Yesterday I read the comics." So, our *Moosepaper* should be red, because he *is* read.

Moosepaper

"All the Print That Fits the Moose,"
The Moosepaper's motto said.
What color shall we make him?
Well, naturally, *read*.

Dwagon - This is a combination of *Dragon* and *Wagon* (like a coaster wagon). Grown-ups think it sounds like cute baby talk to say "Dwagon". Do you?

Revel - A big noisy party. A Friday Revel is a *special* big noisy party to celebrate the last day of school for the week.

Fierce - Able to frighten people. Aunt Rhona's Irish Setter is fierce until he sniffs you and sees how nice you smell.

Dwagon

He was held back in Dragon school
'Cause when he huffed, his tongue stayed cool.
His classmates smoked and burped out flame.
While they got wilder, he stayed tame.
He rolled right past each Friday Revel.
Flunked "Fierce" and "Mean" at freshman level.
Had to leave with handle draggin'.
Could not scare a mouse, poor Dwagon.

Clockodile- This is a combination of *Clock* (what we use to tell time) and *Crocodile* (a rough-skinned animal with a big mouth and lots of teeth).

Ooze - What you feel with your feet at the bottom of a dirty pond.

Slime - Grown-up ooze.

Reptile - A creepy, crawly kind of animal such as a lizard or snake or alligator or crocodile.

Clockodile

Quite early in the dawn of time

He crawled up out of ooze and slime.

With springs and gears and mighty grunts

He measures minutes, days and months.

He ticks and tocks in reptile style,

This never-tardy Clockodile.

Lambp - This is a combination of *Lamb* (a baby sheep), and *Lamp* (like a table lamp).

Ewe - This is what the Mama sheep is called. To make things even more interesting, her name is pronounced so that it rhymes with the word "do" even though it looks like it should be "eee-wee".

Silent "B" - Some words, like lamb, have letters in them which you can *see*, but can't *hear* when you say the word. *Examples:* you don't pronounce the k in knife or the c in scientist. Although this doesn't make much sense, it does help us have fun with words.

Lambp

The Lambp shines brightly so he can see
While looking around for his silent "B".
And then you know what he will do?
Start searching for the "U" in ewe.

Pupperware - This is a take-off on the name of a famous family of food containers designed with tightly fitting lids to store leftover tuna salad, cream of spinach soup and oatmeal until it gets too old to eat and has to be thrown out.

Party animal - Can refer to people who love to get together, make noise, eat pretzels, drink soda pop and play music so loud that the neighbors complain. Or, it can be a term used to describe people who gather at someone's house for a Pupperware party during which time various containers are demonstrated and offered for purchase.

Mess - This is a what happens on your rug if you don't take your puppy out for a walk.

Pupperware

He's a party animal.

Comes in sizes large and small.

With lid on tight, he's quite polite.

He never makes a mess at night.

A pleasant after-dinner guest,

He'll fetch whatever food is left.

Always welcome anywhere

The cute and cuddly Pupperware.

Eraserous Rex - A combination of *Tyrannosaurus Rex* (a big lizard of long ago) and *Eraser* (a thing you use to rub out mistakes).

Ancient - Older than anyone you know. Older than your Grandpa's Grandma. Really old!

Rex - A word, taken from an ancient language, which means "King".

Cursed - When someone has wished bad luck on someone else.

Hex - An exact kind of bad luck. People who are nice (like you and me) do not put curses or hexes on others.

Erasure - A quick wipe-out. What an eraser does.

Glacier - A huge ice cube, bigger than a building, that moves slowly across the land.

Context - Your surroundings or place. The proper context for a noodle is chicken soup.

Eraserous Rex

The ancient Eraserous Rex
Was cursed with a terrible hex.
His one-stroke erasure
Could wipe out a glacier,
Thus leaving him out of context.

Pachythermos - A combination of *Elephant* (which is the common word for Pachyderm) and *Thermos,* (which is a trademarked name for a specially designed bottle to keep drinks hot or cold at school or on a picnic).

Textured - The feeling on the outside of something. Glass has a smooth texture, elephants do not.

Epidermis - A fancy word for the outside skin. For instance, a dermatologist is a skin doctor. An epidermatologist, I suppose, is a skin doctor who works outside.

Pachythermos

How can you tell a Pachythermos?
By his textured epidermis?
Well, while you take some time to think,
Unscrew his nose and have a drink!

Ken Eichenbaum: Visualist

Ken Eichenbaum wanted to be an artist from the time he was a little boy, but his father made him work in the family fruit and vegetable store. By the time he went away to college, he knew that tomatoes and apples and asparagus were okay to eat, but not to manage.

After college some nice men in uniforms told him to join the Army. After he was discharged, he wanted more than ever to become an artist, so he and some friends started an advertising agency. It got very busy, and many people ran back and forth laughing and shouting at each other.

Then he got the idea for *Imaginals*, so he sold his advertising agency and called his friend, Wayne, who went to college with him, and his other friend, Sher, who used to work for his advertising agency.

"They liked the *Imaginals* idea, too," says Mr. Eichenbaum, "and so we met lots of times, and talked on the phone a lot, and called important Saturday morning conferences where we ate buttermilk pancakes with maple syrup, and laughed at each other's ideas until the book was done."

Mr. Eichenbaum lives with his wife Cate, a student chiropractor, in a house next to a ravine in Bayside, Wisconsin.

Wayne Arihood: Versist

Wayne Arihood says, "I love to read, write, eat, and sleep indoors, so I went to college to learn how to do all those things." He earned two degrees: one in English (to improve his reading and writing) and the other in Social Work (so he could get a job, eat, and sleep indoors).

While Mr. Arihood was in college, he met some silly students who worked on the campus humor magazine instead of studying. They persuaded him to divide his time between schoolwork and publishing, and he has never forgiven them for his low grade-point average.

Many years after he graduated, he heard about the *Imaginals*, and he thought, "Hey, that's a great idea I can work on when I'm not doing free-lance writing, running an annual jazz festival, cutting the grass, or watering our dog Satchmo, the pug."

Mr. Arihood's writing style is quite simple, he confesses. "I put all the words and phrases in my computer, and then I hand a hard copy to my wife. She arranges them so they rhyme."

Mr. and Mrs. Arihood live in a house on top of a hill in LaCrosse, Wisconsin, where they play selections from their vast collection of jazz recordings very loudly, and they have few neighbors.

Sher Schachameyer: Illustrator

Sher Schachameyer grew up in St. Louis, Missouri. It took her a long time to go to college because she couldn't quite decide whether to become a philosopher or an artist. By the time she made up her mind, she had earned two degrees and caused her parents and her husband a lot of worry.

Mrs. Schachameyer's husband is more interested in science than in art. They both love to eat good food and argue about politics, and they both love their daughter, Shea, who is good at both science and art.

Mrs. Schachameyer met Mr. Eichenbaum when she was an artist at his advertising agency. Now she works as an artist at the Milwaukee Public Museum, and meets Mr. Eichenbaum and Mr. Arihood on weekends to eat pancakes and work on fun projects together.

When Mrs. Schachameyer worked on the *Imaginals*, her daughter, who was then ten, was her toughest critic. When Shea didn't like something about the art, it was changed. Mrs. Schachameyer hopes that children enjoy reading about *Imaginals* as much as she and Shea enjoyed helping to create *Imaginals*.

The Schachameyers live with their cat in a house with a flower garden in Whitefish Bay, Wisconsin.

Are you a young artist or poet? A person who gets great ideas? Perhaps you can come up with some new *Imaginals* that we can publish. Send your suggestions to Litterati Publishing (address below). If your idea is used you could become famous! We'll credit the idea to you and give you a special prize.

All entries become the property of Litterati, and because we are usually very busy, they cannot be returned. Sorry.

Your name _____

Your age _____

Your address _____

City/State/Zip _____

_____

Was this a classroom project? If so, please fill in the questions below.

Your school _____

School address _____

City/State/Zip _____

_____

Teacher's name _____

Grade _____

Mail to *Imaginals* ®
Litterati Publishing
9470 North Broadmoor Road
Milwaukee, Wisconsin USA 53217

Draw your *Imaginal* here:

Name your *Imaginal*: _____

Write your verse here: _____

_____

_____

_____

_____

_____

_____